Frog and Friends

Written by Eve Bunting

Illustrated by Josée Masse

To my very first granddaughter, Dana Christine Bunting

—Eve

To my friends, Marc and Hélène

—Josée

This book has a reading comprehension level of 2.2 under the ATOS® readability formula.
For information about ATOS please visit www.renlearn.com.
ATOS is a registered trademark of Renaissance Learning, Inc.

Lexile®, Lexile® Framework and the Lexile® logo are trademarks of MetaMetrics, Inc.,
and are registered in the United States and abroad. The trademarks and names of other
companies and products mentioned herein are the property of their respective owners.
Copyright © 2010 MetaMetrics, Inc. All rights reserved.

Sleeping Bear Press™

315 E. Eisenhower Parkway, Ste. 200
Ann Arbor, MI 48108
www.sleepingbearpress.com

Sleeping Bear Press is an imprint of Gale, a part of Cengage Learning.

10 9 8 7 6 5 4 3 2 1

Library of Congress Cataloging-in-Publication Data • Frog and friends / written by Eve Bunting;
• illustrated by Josée Masse. • v. cm. • Summary: Frog and his friends are alarmed by a strange
object that appears on his pond, share a thoughtful--if scratchy--gift, and meet a hippopotamus
that has run away from the zoo. • Contents: Frog goes up, up, up -- Frog's pretty, blue scarf -- •
Frog and hippo. • ISBN 978-1-58536-548-7 (hardcover) -- ISBN 978-1-58536-689-7 (pbk.) • [1.
Frogs--Fiction. 2. Animals--Fiction. 3. Friendship--Fiction. 4. Ponds--Fiction.] I. Masse, Josée, ill.
• II. Title. • PZ7.B91527Fro 2011 • [E]--dc22 • 2010053706

Printed by China Translation & Printing Services Limited, Guangdong Province, China.
Hardcover 1st printing / Softcover 1st printing. 04/2011

Table of Contents

Frog Goes Up, Up, Up

The wind made ripples on Frog's pond.

When he woke up from his sleep he saw

something floating on the water. Something

he had never seen before.

It was BIG, BIG.

It was Orange.

It had a tail.

Frog called his friends. "Come see.

There is a THING in my pond."

"It does not talk. It does not move. It just lies there on the water."

"I think it is a big egg. Maybe a hippopotamus egg," Rabbit said.

"We do not have any hippopotamus-esssss here," Frog told her.

"I think it is a big, big bubble," Possum said.

Frog shook his head, "Who ever heard
of an orange bubble?"

"I think it is a humongous
seed," Raccoon said.

"I think it is a THING with a long, ugly,
skinny tail," Squirrel said.

Frog swam closer.

"Pull its long, ugly, skinny tail," Squirrel said. "Then see what happens."

"Do not," Possum advised. "It might do something bad."

"Be brave," Squirrel urged.

Frog swam closer. He took hold of THING's tail.

Just then the wind came strong. It skidded THING across the pond.

Suddenly THING rose UP, UP, UP.

"Let go! Let go of the tail," Rabbit called.

But Frog was too far above the pond. He was scared to let go.

Rabbit ran for the long, ugly, skinny tail and caught it. She swung behind Frog. They went UP, UP, UP.

Then Squirrel ran and swung behind Rabbit.

Then Possum.

THING began to sink DOWN, DOWN,

DOWN.

Possum's feet were on the ground.

Then Squirrel's.

Then Rabbit's.

Then Frog's.

They fell in a Froggie, Rabbitty, Squirrely,

Possumy heap.

9

THING started to rise again. It bumped

into the oak tree and . . .

BANG!

It was the loudest bang in the world.

Drifting down from the oak tree were little pieces of THING.

"We killed it!" Frog moaned. "Oh, that is so sad."

"We will have a funeral," Rabbit said. "A nice one."

"To show we are sorry," Frog added.

They dug a small hole under the oak tree and buried all the little bits of THING. Then they held paws and sang a sorry song.

"I wonder what THING was?" Rabbit asked.

Frog shook his head. "I suppose we will never know."

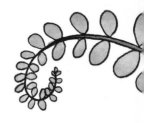

Frog's Pretty Blue Scarf

Raccoon came by Frog's home.

"I was told you have a bad cold," she said. "I knitted this pretty blue scarf for you. It will keep you warm and help your cold."

"Oh, thank you," Frog said. "It will be perfect."

But it was not perfect.

Frog tried to wrap it around his neck.

"But I have no neck," Frog said to himself.

"And I am too slippery."

The scarf slipped up to cover his face.

"Help, help! I cannot breathe."

Then it slipped over his eyes. "Help, help!
Now I cannot see. I will give this pretty
blue scarf to my friend, Rabbit. There is
nothing wasted that you give to a friend."

"Oh, thank you," Rabbit said. "This will be perfect."

She wore the scarf all day.

But it was not perfect.

"My own fur is so soft and cozy. This pretty blue scarf makes me too hot. I will give it to my friend, Squirrel. He will look spiffy in it."

Squirrel did look spiffy in it. "This is perfect," he said.

But it was not perfect.

"This pretty blue scarf is scratchy," he said. "It makes me itch. I know, I will give it to my friend, Possum. She can cuddle her babies in it."

"Oh, thank you," Possum said. "This will be perfect."

She tucked her babies in the pretty blue scarf.

But it was not perfect.

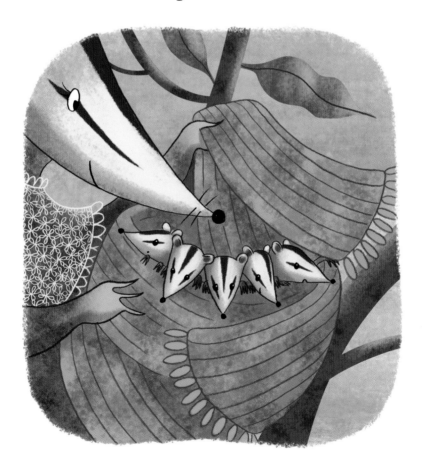

Her babies did not like it one bit.

"Let us out, let us out," they squeaked.

"Help, help! We are trapped."

They squeaked and squealed and bit

their mother and each other.

"Oh dear," Possum said, untucking

them. "I know. I will give the pretty blue

scarf to Frog. I hear he has a bad cold."

Frog was surprised when Possum came.

"Thank you, Possum," he said. "But I

am too slippery to wear a pretty blue scarf.

And I have no neck. A scarf will not stay

where I put it."

"Mmm," Possum said. "Let me think."

She put the scarf on Frog. She tied the

long ends around Frog's fat belly. "There,"

she said, "now it will stay where you put it."

"Thank you," Frog said. "You are so

clever."

Possum nodded. "That is true. I am glad I gave it to you. There is nothing wasted that you give to a friend."

"That is what I always say," Frog told her.

When Possum left he sat down and wrote a thank-you note to Raccoon.

"I feel better already," he wrote. "I am wearing the pretty blue scarf and it is perfect. Absolutely perfect."

Frog and Hippo

Frog was resting on a lily pad when he

heard a noise.

CRUNCH, CRUNCH, CLUMP. CLUMP, CRUNCH, CRUNCH.

He hopped quickly into his pond and

peered over the edge.

Something was coming. Something BIG.

"Hello," a big voice said.

"Hello," Frog stammered. "Who are you?"

"I am Hippopotamus."

Frog quaked. This must be the biggest

animal in the world. He had heard of

hippopotamus-esssss. But this was the

first one he had seen.

Oh no, he thought. He has come for his egg which we killed and buried.

Frog took a deep breath, "If you have come for your egg, Hippopotamus, we killed it. We did not mean to. We are very sorry."

"I do not know what you mean," Hippopotamus said. "I do not lay eggs. I am a mammal."

"Oh." Frog was not sure what that meant. But he was happy that Hippopotamus was not angry. He was so **BIG**.

"Just call me Hippo," Hippopotamus said. "I live in town in the Little Zoo. Someone left my cage open. I ran away to see the world. Then I saw your pond. I like ponds. May I join you?"

"Of course." Frog moved over.

Hippo waddled in. He was so **BIG**

he filled the pond.

Hippo closed his eyes. "Lovely!"

Frog could not even stretch his legs.

"Will you stay long?" he asked.

"Mmm," Hippo said. "This is so nice.

I think I will stay forever."

Frog gulped. "But there is not room

for both of us."

"Oh, you are so small. I think we will

both fit."

Frog did not want to share his pond. How could he swim with BIG Hippo in the water? He liked to dance around his pond in the moonlight. With no one to watch. How could he do that if Hippo stayed forever? How could he have quiet time for his nap? He did not want to tell Hippo to go away. That would be rude.

Frog looked up. Geese were flying south for winter.

Oh yes, Frog thought.

"Hippo," he said, "soon it will be winter.
Look! The geese are flying south. The pond
will be covered with ice. It will be so cold.
I will be having my winter sleep in the mud
on the bottom. But you are too big to cover
yourself with that mud. There will be ice,
ice, ice all around you."

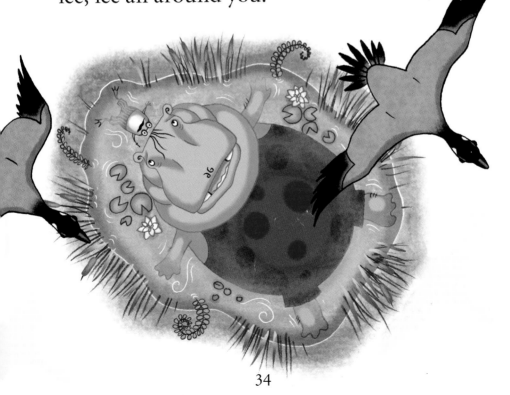

"Oh my!" Hippo said. "You are right. And I hate to be cold." He shivered and the pond water sloshed over the side. Ants ran for cover. "They do keep my pond warm at the Little Zoo," Hippo said. "And they give me warm straw to lie in. It is pretty nice back there."

"Sometimes you have to run away to see what the world is like," Frog said. "But sometimes you are happy to go home."

"That is true," Hippo said. "I liked being with you. But I think I will go back now."

"Goodbye," Frog said. "Nice to meet you." Then, happy once more, he swam round and round his pond.

After that he took a nap.